Shumshere Singh

The Maharaja of Patiala on the Frontier

With an introd. Giving a Brief Summary of Lord Elgin's Administration

Shumshere Singh

The Maharaja of Patiala on the Frontier
With an introd. Giving a Brief Summary of Lord Elgin's Administration

ISBN/EAN: 9783337142902

Printed in Europe, USA, Canada, Australia, Japan

Cover: Foto ©Andreas Hilbeck / pixelio.de

More available books at **www.hansebooks.com**

The Maharaja of Patiala on the Frontier.

BY

SHUMSHERE SINGH,

Aitmad-ud-Daulah, Iftikhar-ul-Mulk, Sirdar Bahadur, Private Secretary to His Highness the Maharaja of Patiala.

With an Introduction giving a Brief Summary of Lord Elgin's Administration.

———

1899.

———

W. Newman & Co.,
4 Dalhousie Square, Calcutta.

PRINTED BY W. NEWMAN & CO.
AT THE CAXTON PRESS, 1/2 MISSION ROW, CALCUTTA

TO

HIS MOST KIND AND NOBLE MASTER

His Highness Farzand-i-Khas-i-Daulat-i-Inglishia,

Mansur-i-Zaman, Amir-ul-Umara,

Maharaja-Dhiraj Rajeshwar Sri Maharaja-i-Rajgan

Sir Rajindra Singh, Mahindra Bahadur,

Maharaja of Patiala,

G. C. S. I.

THIS BOOK IS HUMBLY DEDICATED

BY THE AUTHOR

AS A TOKEN OF DEEP RESPECT, LOYALTY, AND ADMIRATION.

PREFACE.

THE following pages are compiled with the aid of my office files and the cuttings from newspapers that I keep in my office. They do not profess to have any literary finish, or to give a complete account of the frontier operations in which His Highness the Maharaja took a prominent part. They only deal with what concerned the Maharaja,—the hard work he underwent and the high honors which followed.

The importance of sport as an imperial factor is often lost sight of, and its influence is not always considered to extend beyond the confines of the playing fields. But it was on the playing fields of Eton, the Duke of Wellington once said, that the battle of Waterloo was won, and the destinies of nations decided. That sport is not without its use, that, in fact, it is an essential feature, in the training of our Indian Princes has been proved to demonstration by the recent action of His Highness the Maharaja which forms the subject of the following pages. The sporting prince is not necessarily a prince whose whole thought is absorbed in the pursuit of pleasure to be derived from

PREFACE.

sport. He can also be a prince who, while culti-
vating the manly habits on the turf, is not unmindful of his duties as a ruler. While he is unques-
tionably the prince who can readily engage, with
credit to himself and his country, in the rough
game of war in defence of the interests of the Empire. Such is the Maharaja of Patiala, and such he
is acknowledged to be by all who have had an
opportunity to come in actual contact with him.
With all his soldierly qualities, he is the most
modest and unassuming of men, and hates nothing
so much as parade and display.

The loyalty of the Patiala State, and its services
to the British Government in time of need in the
past are a matter of history, and need not be re-
counted here. That the present Ruler of Patiala
has " worthily sustained the credit for loyalty of
the State and the Chief of Patiala " has been
admitted by Lord Elgin's Government, which has
been an appreciative Government after all. In
the introduction I have given a brief summary of
the salient points of Lord Elgin's Administration
as Viceroy and Governor-General of India.

CALCUTTA: SHUMSHERE SINGH.
3rd January, 1899.

CONTENTS.

INTRODUCTION ... ... i to xv

CHAPTER I—The Frontier Campaign ... 1 to 9

CHAPTER II—The Mohmand Expedition—What led up to it—Despatch of the Patiala Imperial Service Troops—His Highness proceeds in person to the Frontier—Advance against the Mohmands ... ... 10 to 27

CHAPTER III—The end of the Mohmand Expedition—Return of His Highness the Maharaja to Patiala ... ... 28 to 38

CHAPTER IV—Reduction in the Tirah Expeditionary Force and return of the Imperial Service Troops ... ... 39 to 54

CHAPTER V—Imperial Recognition of the Patiala Services ... ... 55 to 66

CHAPTER VI—The Star of India .. . 67 to 78

CHAPTER VII—His Excellency the Viceroy's visit to Patiala and Investiture of His Highness the Maharaja ... 79 to 107

INTRODUCTION.

AFTER a wise, kind and powerful rule of five years over this vast peninsula, consisting of various creeds and castes of people, so very divergent in manners, customs and religious faith, H. E. Lord Elgin, our Viceroy and Governer-General, is on the eve of his departure for his happy home. I need not mention that every administration, like the present, had two sides, and every reign has had its supporters and opponents. This division of opinion in political matters must always exist. The administration of Lord Elgin does not form an exception to this general rule. It has its supporters and detractors as well. To the supporter I have nothing more to say: but to those of our countrymen, who have not been impressed with the good shade of Lord Elgin's reign, I have a few words to vouchsafe. The spirit *nil admirari* is never a sign of healthy progress, and it is not well for a man to see always the dark sides of a character.

As an official of the Patiala State, I had the honor of coming in contact closely with His Excellency's administration, and am grateful to him for the honor that His Excellency has been pleased to bestow on our Maharaja. And as an Indian I consider it my duty to try to remove, as far as lies in my power, the misgivings of my countrymen regarding Lord Elgin's Indian administration. Before I describe in detail the relationship between His Excellency's *régime* and the Patiala State, which is the purpose of this small *brochure*, I shall give an outline of his general administration in India. At the outset I must mention that very few of us are alive to the many difficulties that lie in the way of such an important position as the Viceroy and Governor-General of India. We are apt to find fault with an administration because we cannot realize the responsibility and difficulties of the situation. It is for this incapability that many of us become altogether blind to the bright side of an administration. The same remark may be brought home to the detractor of Lord Elgin's administration.

No administration of a Viceroy and Governor-General of India has been visited by so many unforeseen calamities as that of Lord Elgin. Numberless misfortunes, one after another, swept over the length and breadth of the country in rapid succession. Famine, plague, earthquake, rioting and frontier troubles shook the empire to its very foundations. A single one of this heavy and dire list of calamities is quite enough to tax the energies and attention of a ruler to its

highest stretch. But Lord Elgin had
not to combat one enemy, but quite a
number of them. He had not only to
send an army to quell the disturbances
caused by a mad fakir, but had to fight
against God's visitations for the life and
prosperity of the people entrusted to his
care. In the very beginning of his
career Western India suffered from the
dreadful plague, and Bombay, the finest
port and city of India, was on the verge
of ruin. Before he could prevent the
fell disease from spreading all over the
country, the whole of India was visited by
a dreadful famine. Such a widespread
scarcity no other Indian ruler had to face.
Some of them no doubt displayed wonderful administrative powers in quelling
famine, which was in one and every case
a provincial calamity. Their battle was
a fight against the enemy of one particular
province. Lord Elgin's war has, however,
been against a number of enemies. Dur-

ing his *régime* not one single province was affected by famine, but the whole of India. He had to spend money, concert measures and devote his whole-minded attention to suppress this widespread famine. And no sooner was he nearly successful in this, than Bengal and Assam suffered from a terrible earthquake, which made a number of people altogether homeless. We need not recount the sufferings of the people from those calamities, for they are still fresh in their memory. We do not know how many have been gathered to their forefathers by famine and plague, and how heavily the number roll of widows and orphans has swelled in India. What we mean particularly to say is about the various wise and good measures introduced by Lord Elgin for coping with these calamities. This will clearly show the extraordinary power of organisation, the superior administrative talent, and the good and kind heart which Lord Elgin has. But for the way in which he introduced various means for suppressing plague, spent money for stopping famine, and afforded relief to the famine-stricken millions, India would have by this time presented a dreadful prospect of a desolate country. It may be that some of the agents appointed to carry out the remedial measures did not prove true to their duties. But the ruler is not to blame for the shortcomings of the people engaged by him, for Lord Elgin always took notice of their malconduct whenever he was informed of it. It is the intention which should be the test of one's own actions. And is there any man in India who, with his conscience clean, can say that Lord Elgin had not the best of motives to do what he did for India? The measures which Lord Elgin's Government adopted for repressing the

plague might have been a little too harsh
in some places, but have they not been
crowned with success in all other places ?
Has not the Government done much to
put a stop to the spread of the disease in
other parts of India ? Isolated cases of
miscarriage of justice do not prove the
absence of utility of a general rule
Whenever any law or regulation is
brought into force, one or two men
occasionally suffer, either from want of
experience on the part of the agents
employed, or the bad nature of some of
them. But the head of the administration
should not be blamed for the frail and
occasional shortcomings, if the measure,
as a whole, proves beneficial to the
country at large. Is any one prepared
to say that plague rules enunciated under
Lord Elgin's wise and kind advice
have not done good to the country ?
And has not Lord Elgin dealt strongly
with the offenders ? The mild nature

of the operation of plague rules in the Metropolis of India sufficiently proves that Lord Elgin always cared for the comfort and convenience of the people, and that all his measures were actuated by the best of motives When the plague suddenly appeared in Bombay, the Government was surprised, and could not at once arrive at a definite plan of work. And hence were some of the hardships to which people were subject. But the mild and wise way in which measures had been meted out subsequently in other parts of the country, speaks volumes in favour of the administrative ability of Lord Elgin, and his desire to respect the feelings and sentiments of the people.

The next most important incident of Lord Elgin's administration is the famine operation organised by his Government. There is one universal voice all over the country in favour of the wise and kind

measures adopted by Lord Elgin to suppress the famine. He worked day and
night, visited from place to place, debated
with his councillors, spent every limited
resource at his disposal, nay, even appeal-
ed to the generosity of the nations of
the world, to give food to the starving
millions of India. He spared himself
neither care nor comfort to save the
poor. He spent many sleepless nights
to concert remedial measures. And
at last he succeeded in repressing the
terrible famine. Is he not therefore
entitled to our deep gratitude and ve-
neration for this single act of unflinching
devotion to the cause of suffering
humanity ? Will the people of India
ever forget him who saved them from
death and misery ? The only charge
that some fastidious critics bring against
Lord Elgin's Government in this connection is that he was too late to take up
the operation of relief. They say that

Lord Elgin did not pay any attention when the whole country was speaking of famine, and famine. A little thought and consideration will convince this class of critics that an administrator like the Viceroy and Governor-General of India cannot wed himself to any work without being sufficiently convinced of its necessity and nature. He could not at once enter into work of famine relief, because he did not get official reports on the subject. He was late because he required a few days to understand for himself correctly the true nature of things, and to lay down a definite plan of action. He was late, a little no doubt, but experience and final result shows that it has done no harm, and the subsequent successful and efficient famine measures were the outcome of this wise deliberation and correctness of information.

Similarly, in coping with the damages

done by the earthquake, Lord Elgin's Government has been sufficiently equal. It has spent a considerable amount of money, and is still doing, in restoring the many public buildings that were levelled to the ground. The various measures adopted for repressing the famine and the spread of plague, when looked at impartially, distinctly show the ability and heart of Lord Elgin. This work alone is quite sufficient to keep Lord Elgin's reign engraven on the mind of the people.

A few words will not be out of place here regarding the Sedition Act, which is looked upon by many as a most retrograde measure, which a civilized Government should not adopt. It is a bug-bear to the political aspirants of our country, who have been crying aloud that by this unwise legislation of Lord Elgin's Government our political advancement has receded a century back. To pronounce an impartial verdict on this question, we must not look upon it with a jaundiced eye. Every right-thinking man will admit that some of our lip-deep patriots have done more harm than good by their unguarded utterances and writings. Education in India has not reached that scale which it has done in other countries of the world. The masses of our country are still in that dark ignorance which they were centuries before. And although some of them have received a smattering of English education, they have not however received that political training which will enable them to regard all measures of the Government in their proper light. In this infant state of their political life and culture they must not be suffered to be imbued with false notions of freedom and political right. The various leaders of our political movements have not been sufficiently

wise in training our young men. They
have inspired them with many new-fang-
led ideas of political right, which have
created a number of idle talkers in the
country, who, in and out of season, speak
ill of any measure adopted by the Government. Such a state of things is
highly detrimental to our advancement,
and any measure that is intended as a
check for this growing spirit of disaffec-
tion and fault-finding, should be regarded
as a real boon by them who have the
well-being of the country and rising ge-
neration at heart. What led Lord Elgin
to think of such an Act? Was not the
affair in the Bombay Presidency sufficient
enough for the adoption of a stringent
measure? Rioting became the order of
the day. The Hindus and Mussulmans
fought with one another in metropolitan
towns without any fear and dread of the
Police. The race prejudices of the ignorant masses were fanned by unthinking and

so-called leaders of the community. Irresponsible editors did not shrink from preaching any amount of sedition in their papers. These irresponsible and careless writings told greatly upon the mind of the ignorant masses. This sort of dangerous feeling—this haphazard and careless way of criticising the Government measures—grew so very terrible gradually, that at last some of the fanatics did not hesitate to murder some innocent officers of the State. Was not Lord Eigin's Government, I ask, sufficiently justified in introducing a measure that would put a stop to such things in future? If we look upon the Sedition Act without any bias or prejudice, we cannot but be impressed that the measure is very opportune and a wholesome antidote against the feeling of growing discontentment and unrest. The Government does not object to our representing our grievances and declaring our views about their ways and actions. What it wants is that we must do so in a decent way, and we must be well-guarded in our utterances and writings This Sedition Act, in my view, will give a better training to our young men, and we will ere long have a class of sensible writers and speakers, who will be alive to the responsibilities attached to their position, and crush down the feeling of discontent and dissatisfaction. *

The other most important political act of Lord Elgin's Government is the frontier campaign. It is an imperial question that has been engaging the attention of one statesman after another. That the frontier tribes should be kept in subjection for the safety of India will be sufficiently proved from the account that follows in the next chapter.

---

* To my countrymen who are discontented with this Act, I may only say that they should turn the pages of history and see what Aurangzebe did.

CHAPTER I.

THE FRONTIER CAMPAIGN.

BEFORE I describe the causes that led to the frontier campaign, I will show that for the safety of the Indian Government the mad tribes should always be kept in check. India is well protected by nature on all sides against any foreign invasion. On all sides, except the north, she is walled by the sea, and England is so well known for her naval power that none would dare meet her in water. The only opening that can lead a foreign army to India is through the northern pass. It is through this pass the hordes of invaders came and overran India. Babar, Timur, Mahomed Ghoi, Nader Shah and others took advantage of this pass and attacked India. This is the weak point in the defence of India, and should Russia or any other power come to India, she must come through this narrow defile.

It is, therefore, a matter of very great imperial importance that the tribes living around the frontier hills should be either friendly with the British Government or kept in perpetual awe and restraint. To send out a strong army, therefore, for subduing the tribes of the frontier under the Mad Fakir was an imperial necessity with Lord Elgin. The safety of the Government and the protection of the British prestige necessitated this campaign.

The great tribal upheaval of 1897 is the necessary sequel of the Chitral Expedition. The retention of British troops at Chitral, though repudiated by Lord Rosebery's Government for a short while, was however approved by Lord Salisbury from great imperial interest. The occupation and retention of Chitral has not been without any benefit to the people. During the two years that the British flag had floated over Chakdara and Malakand

trade had greatly flourished in the Swat
Valley. For two years no disturbance
was caused by the people, and no in-
jury was done to the British officers.
The barbarous people around improved
greatly within a short time by coming in
contact with a powerful civilization.
One class of people, however, did not like
the approach of the British power. Advance of civilization and spread of education dissipates prevailing superstitions
and prejudices. And the priesthood loses
all its control when people grow enlightened and educated. The priests of
the Afghan border did not therefore like
the Chitral road. The Mullahs therefore
began to work upon the people, who were
by nature ignorant and fanatical, and
their mission was greatly helped by the
victory of the Turks over the Greeks and
the publication of the Amir's book on
Jehad, who, the Government knows well,
is whether a friend or enemy. The foolish

people grew excited and wanted to wage a crusade. They were in need of a leader, and they got a powerful one in the Mad Mullah. The fanatics made great preparations, and all their movements were concealed to the British officers. This fanatical movement in Upper Swat was not noticed until the early days of July, and even then his power was a secret. In the name of religion, the Mad Fakir declared a holy war against the infidel. To produce an impression on the people he began to work miracles. People brought him offerings of food and money, and accordingly his stores were greatly replenished. He said that he was invisible at night, and people found him so. He declared that he stood in need of no body's help, for he alone would go to heaven. He devised various means to work upon the credulity of the people, and he succeeded. The Mad Fakir kept all his armies concealed in mountainous fastnesses, and ordered that no one should approach a particular hill, lest the heavenly host might be prematurely revealed. Rumours ran like wildfire, and the British officers could not but ultimately believe that a great danger was hovering upon them.

On the afternoon of the 26th July, Major Deane reported to Brigadier-General Meiklejohn, who commanded the Malakand garrison, that the Mad Mullah had collected a large armed gathering, and an attack was possible. He at once wired to Mardan to march instantly. At 8-30 Lieutenant P. Elliot Lockhart received the order, and at 1-30 A.M. they began to march. All preparations were quickly made, and the Commanding Officer soon got the correct information that the Fakir had passed Khar. Then began the great and long talked of campaign. The expedition first worked in Upper Swat, for the Mad Fakir created

troubles first in that quarter. The British
soldiers and officers displayed wonderful
ability in relieving and defending Chakdara, and this powerful expedition was
terminated on the 26th of August.

The next was the advance against
Mohmands, and it was in this expedition
that the Maharaja of Patiala himself took
his army and fought against the enemies of the Paramount Power. Before I
describe the services of the Patiala troops
in the frontier expedition, I should say
what has this campaign shown. Within
this short time the frontier tribes have
come to their senses and have understood
that the British Government is too strong
for them. Their hallucinations have all
disappeared, and they have been making
overtures for peace. The public have also
been convinced that for the future safety
of the empire the position of the British
troops should be consolidated in the frontier, and a strong army with good roads,

forts and telegraphic communications should be always kept there.

Our neighbours in the frontier are not a good and honest set of people. They are a lot of fanatic and wild rebels. They can, at any time, for their convenience, introduce enemies through their territories to our country. Honesty and fair play is at discount with them. They have no ideas of a civilized Government, and they have false notions of liberty and indepen-dence. To keep them in control and to prevent them from making raids in the British cities requires the presence of a strong and powerful army, with able and intelligent officers. Fear is the only means by which they will remain peace-ful. Thus, from a political point of view, the campaign was a necessity. It was not undertaken at the whim of an officer, but was the outcome of circumstances over which the Indian Government had no control. An administrator, if he really wishes to make his Government powerful, must always keep in restraint the wild rebels. Ignorant people do not understand the real essence of affairs. They must be punished for their offence and properly watched.

Another most important issue of this campaign is that the loyalty of the Indian chiefs to the British throne has been sufficiently proved. The British Government has been convinced that should an occasion arise, the Indian chiefs would place their army and resources at the disposal of the Sovereign Power. A number of Indian chiefs not only sent their armies to the frontier, but many of them personally went to the field to fight against the enemies of the Queen-Empress. Of these loyal Indian chiefs, H. H. the Maharaja of Patiala is one who himself, with his troops, rendered brilliant service in the frontier. Lord Elgin's Government has happily solved a great and difficult imperial problem whether the Indian chiefs are friendly towards the Suzerain Power, and has strengthened greatly the relation between the Paramount Power and its allies by recognizing properly and in a becoming manner the services of the various chiefs. The Patiala people are particularly thankful to His Excellency for the honor he has conferred upon their ruler.

CHAPTER II.

THE tidal wave of fanaticism, rising in
the Tochi Valley, was sweeping down the
frontier, and had influenced the Mohmands, as all other border tribes. What
the Mad Fakir was doing in Swat and
Buner, the Hadda Mullah was doing here.
The Mullah is an Afghan by origin. His
name is Najm-ud-din, and he is called
the Hadda Mullah, after Hadda, a village
of Afghanistan, the Mullah's home and
birthplace. Thirteen years ago he fell
out with the Amir, and was obliged to
retire to the independent Mohmand territory, where he has lived ever since. He
is known to be a man of eloquence, and
this, combined with his sanctity, seems

to have given him a strong power over
the border tribes.   Like all other Mullahs, he is no friend of the British Power,
which is " infidel" after all, and he looks
with fear on the advance of the infidel into
the sacred region of Muhammadanism.
In 1895 he sent the fighting men of
the Mohmands to resist the Chitral
Expeditionary Force, and has since been
fanning and keeping alive the fire of discontent and fanaticism, which, though a
constant feature with the border tribes,
received a fresh impetus during the
Chitral Expedition.

The bazars of India, like the London
coffee-houses of the last century, are always full of marvellous tales, which no
infrequently contain the germ of truth
Vague rumours had for some time pa
been current in the bazars of Shanka
garh that something was going to happen,
which foreboded no good to the authorities and to the inhabitants of the village.

A few days previous to August 8th, 1897,
the Hindu *banniahs* of Shankargarh de-
serted their bazar, came flying to Peshawar, and gave out that their village was
in danger of being raided and plundered
by the Mohmands. And before the
authorities at Peshawar had time to send
out reinforcements to Shabkadar, Shabkadar fort had been attacked, Shankargarh had been burnt, and the Mohmands
had taken up a strong position on the
plateau befor the fort. Next day, on the
9th of August, the Mohmands gave
battle to Colonel Woon, who had moved
out to attack them, but being charged by
the cavalry under General Elles, who
had arrived from Peshawar during the
engagement, got demoralized, and fled to
the hills in disorder.

This deliberate violation of the British territory by the Mohmands necessitated the organization of a campaign
against them, and the Governor-General

in Council sanctioned it. The general plan of the operations, as arranged by the Commander-in-Chief, was as follows:—

1. Sir Bindon Blood, with two brigades of the Malakand Field Force and due proportions of cavalry and guns, was to move through South Bajaur to Nawagai, and on the 15th of September invade the Mohmand country from that place.

2. On the same date Major-General Elles, with an equal force, would leave Shabkadar, and entering the mountains, march north-east to effect a junction.

3. This having been done, the combined forces, under the supreme command of Sir Bindon Blood, would be brought back through the Mohmands' territories to Shabkadar. Incidentally they would deal with the Hadda Mullah's village of Jarobi, and inflict such punishment on the tribesmen as might be necessary to ensure their submission.

This was the time for the Patiala State
to come forward with its wonted loyalty
to press upon the Government the services of its Imperial Service Troops.
This it did, and the Governor-General in
Council resolved " that the time has
come when the assistance of the troops,
so loyally prepared and maintained, may
be accepted from the Chiefs of the Punjab, and when they may be allowed to
co-operate in punishing those who have
made, and are making, persistent efforts
to disturb the peace of that province.
It is impossible to employ cavalry to any
great extent in the expeditions which have
now been undertaken ; the Governor-
General in Council has therefore decided
to accept from the States in the Punjab
the services of four battalions of infantry
and of two companies of sappers and
miners. Those troops will immediately
proceed to the front."

This Resolution of the Government

of India was hailed with delight in Patiala, and the 1st Patiala Regiment, with
necessary transport and accompanied by
Captain Cox and Lieutenant Davidson,
at once left for service in two special
trains at noon on the 6th September,
1898, to take their place in the divisional
troops of the Mohmand Field Force
under Major-General Elles at Peshawar.
His Highness the Maharaja happened to
be at Kasauli at the time, and, being un-
able to personally address the troops on
their departure, wired Captain Cox at
Patiala, wishing him and the regiment
the best of luck and success, and asking
him to tell the regiment that he congratulated them on their first service
in the field, and that he hoped they
would give the best account of themselves
wherever their services might be required
by the Government.

But this was not enough for a loyal
Prince like the Maharaja of Patiala.

His instincts of loyalty were not satisfied with merely despatching a regiment of his troops. They prompted him to proceed in person to the frontier and there lead his whole army against the enemies of the British Empire. Accordingly, on the 6th of September, the very day when the 1st Patiala Regiment was leaving for service, His Highness wired His Honor the Lieutenant-Governor of the Punjab, requesting His Honor to ask His Excellency the Viceroy's permission for him to go to the frontier with the whole of his Imperial Service Troops and lead them against the enemy wherever they could be of most service to the Government. Reply came from the Lieutenant-Governor by wire on the 10th, at 8 o'clock in the night, and it was this :—
" Your Highness' telegram of 6th instant. Orders of Government India just received, it is not practicable to utilize the whole of Your Highness' troops or to

arrange that Your Highness should lead
in person the regiment sent. Government
India will be glad to meet your wish to
go to the front in this way, *viz.*, to attach
Your Highness to General Elles' staff with
a field troop of Patiala Imperial Service
Lancers as personal escort. General
Elles leaves Shabkadar, 18 miles from
Peshawar, on 13th, so Your Highness
should join him forthwith if you wish to
accompany him."

There was no question of the wish of
His Highness. He wished to proceed
in person to the frontier, and there try
to do what he could by his personal
services in defence of Her Majesty's
Indian Empire. The capacity in which
he was to do that did not matter much
to him. But then he had only two days
to reach from Kasauli to Shabkadar.
There was no time to be lost. That very
night, therefore, preparations were made
for His Highness' departure from Kasauli,

and the next morning His Highness left for Patiala. Here His Highness stopped for a few hours, and after seeing that the field troop and every other arrangement was all right, left again for Peshawar by special train. On reaching Lahore, it became known that owing to the line being blocked on account of the heavy rush for the frontier, the special could not run further. A local train for Rawalpindi was about to start from Lahore, and it was arranged that the Maharaja's saloon be attached to the local, and be thus carried to Rawalpindi, from where another special was to carry it to Peshawar. Thus His Highness the Maharaja, attended by only the officers of his staff—the rest, including the field troop of the Imperial service Lancers, had to be left behind for want of railway accommodation—reached Peshawar by special train at 7 A.M. on the 13th of September. General Gaselee, with other officers, was present on the platform to receive His Highness. A guard-of-honor, with band and colours, was also present, and His Highness was received with due honours. A nice little bungalow just in front of the railway station had been engaged by the Government authorities for the accommodation of His Highness. Here the Maharaja breakfasted, and after resting awhile, sent out General Phitam Singh, Colonels Hira Singh and Chand Singh of his staff, and Lt.-Col. C. W. Owen, C.M.G., C.I.E., with horses and transport to Shabkadar; while he himself drove out in a tum-tum, attended by Major Siva Singh of his staff, and escorted by some Sowars, whom General Gaselee had sent for this purpose, as the field troop of the Imperial Service Lancers had not yet arrived.

On reaching Shabkadar, His Highness received a very hearty welcome from

General Elles, and learnt that the movements from that place had been deferred
till the 15th. That morning General
Elles had inspected General Macgregor's
Brigade (2nd), which comprised, among
others, the 1st Patiala Infantry. The
Patiala Sikhs had called forth admiration
on every side. They were considered as
fine a body of the great fighting race as
one could have wished to see, and it had
been pleasing to note that under the
inspection they had been as self-con-
trolled and confident as if it had not
been their first appearance on active
service. They were safe to fulfil the
high opinion already formed of their
military efficiency. General Westmacott's
Brigade was inspected the following
morning, and orders for the advance
were out.

The advance commenced on the 15th.
The 1st Brigade led the way at 5-30 A.M.,
and were shortly followed by a portion

of the 2nd Brigade, escorting about 1,300
camels, loaded with kits and stores.
Owing, however, to the Hadda Mullah
being reported to be in force about eight
miles from Shabkadar, the hills on either
side of the path had to be crowned by
the flankers of the 20th Punjab Infantry, who were acting as Advance Guard,
and the advance was necessarily very
slow. After proceeding about seven miles
to a village called Daud, the road was
found to lead up a precipitous defile
hardly passable for mules and quite im-
practicable for camels. And from this
point began what has been called one of
the most trying marches that troops ever
made in India. The heat of the sun, as
the day advanced, was simply terrific,
and the path was simply a track across
slippery sheet rock, over which the mules
mounted to the top by a series of jumps
and acrobatic feats. This defile was the
place where the Hadda Mullah was ex-

pected to offer resistance, and numerous
sangars had been built commanding
bends in the road. Whether, however,
his heart failed him, or whether the news
of General Blood's advance from the
north had induced him to retire, is not
obvious, but there is no doubt that if he
had held the defile, as he evidently first
intended to do, he would not have been
ejected without considerable loss on both
sides.

As it was, however, the steep ascent of
the Karapa had been made, and the
Gandab Plateau gained, the same day
that the advance from Shabkadar commenced, and without the slightest resistance being offered by the enemy. And
now were made a series of reconnais-
sances up the Jarobi road, to the Khopak
and over the Nabaki Passes, and, beyond
these, up to Kung, towards Nawagai, and
towards Danish Kol. But there was no
sign visible of an enemy in force in any

of the numerous fortified posts that commanded every spur on the hills around.
They were apparently engaged in oppos-
ing the advance of General Blood from
the north, which they feared most. The
reconnaissance which General Westmacott pushed out to the Nabaki Pass found
helio connection with General Blood's
division, and the helio brought the news
that the enemy were hanging about the
entrenchments of General Blood's Camp,
and that the General's force was rather
pressed for food.

A conjunction with General Blood was
imperative, and General Elles marched
out from Nabaki on the morning of
the 21st of September, with General
Westmacott's Brigade, for Lakarai, which
is five miles from Nawagai, where General Blood was encamped with General
Wodehouse's Brigade: Brigadier-General Macgregor remaining at Nabaki to
defeat any possible movement of the

enemy. Exactly at a quarter past ten, Generals Blood and Elles met in a tope of trees, and there was a general hand-shaking as the two staffs met. There was plenty of news from the Nawagai Column, for they confirmed the news that the enemy were in force at Badmanai. Their camp had been most vigorously attacked the preceding evening.

General Blood soon returned to his camp at Nawagai, and the next morning, while General Westmacott's Brigade advanced up he Badmani Valley from Lakarai, Colonel Graves, who had as-sumed command of Colonel Wodehouse's Brigade—Colonel Wodehouse having been wounded during the attack on the Nawagai Column the preceding evening —advanced similarly from Nawagai. The enemy were found in force upon all the spurs which covered the advance to the Badmanai Pass, and the day having too for advanced to carry the pass, General Elles and the two Brigades encamped at the foot of the pass, near a village called Kuzchinarai.

At seven in the morning the two Brigades fell in to assault, and marched simultaneously. The first objective was a low, conical hill, and a village at the mouth of the pass, which was found on approach to be occupied by the enemy. General Westmacott was entrusted with the turning of this position, and after some severe fighting the pass was carried.

That night the Brigade encamped at Badmanai village. From Badmanai the force moved down to Sorakhwa, and on the morning of the 26th marched out of the fort there to punish the Jarobi Valley—General Elles and staff, including His Highness the Maharaja, accompanying the advanced guard. The country around presented a most desolate and arid appearance, and there wa

nowhere to be seen the valley of the Mohmands, which 'overflows with milk and
honey." But the Patiala Cavalry, which
were furnishing the advanced scouts,
came back and reported a gorge, and this
was the promised land. A reconnaissance up this gorge was fired on by the
enemy on the heights on either side, but
they were soon dispersed. The force
then advanced, and a square tower standing prominently in the centre of the
waterway showed where the valley opened
out to the right, into the Jarobi Valley
proper, the home of the Hadda Mullah·
The sappers advanced and applied the
fatal torch to Jarobi, and yet there was
no hostile demonstration. Then suddenly, when the road became still narrower,
a blaze of fire was poured in from either
side, and it was evident that the defile
was held by the enemy in force. The
artillery was now brought into action,
and in a few minutes the whole of the

valley was in flames, and the main object of the expedition had been attained.

There is a good story told that, during the attack on the Badmanai Pass, the Hadda Mullah was seen personally riding among the flying foe, but his pony fell in an awkward place, and they put him into a litter and carried him off. There were women close by, refugees from the villages, who cursed him in their choicest tongue for the troubles he had brought upon them.

With the capture of the Badmanai Pass, and the assault on Jarobi, the fighting stage of the operations may be said to have been brought to a close on the 28th September.

CHAPTER III.

THERE was now no prospect of further
fighting. The military part of the expedition was over. The Hadda Mullah
had fled across the Afghan boundary, his
spell had been broken, the Mohmands
had been taught a sharp lesson, their
country had been swept through by the
Sirkar's forces, and their *purdah* had
been lifted. It was only the "political
walk round" that now remained, and for
this no troops were required. The troops
under General Elles, therefore, moved
back in separate columns to Peshawar to
rest there until they were called on for
active service again. His Highness the
Maharaja also, with General Elles' permission, now left the scene of war, and
a telegram from him, dated Nabaki,

the 28th of September, brought the welcome news to the people of Patiala that His Highness was at last returning home, sale and sound, from the frontier.

It need not be mentioned here how eagerly the people of Patiala watched the course of events on the frontier, where their young and beloved master was sharing all the hardships of service like a common soldier. Every day that passed increased their anxiety for their noble prince, who, though so young, was still prepared to emulate the manly deeds of his ancestors. True, they knew that the British officers who conducted the expedition would help the Maharaja, who had set so noble an example to the Indian princes, to go through the ordeal uninjured. True also, every now and then, a telegram from His Highness or a paragraph in some daily brought them the assurance that all went well with the expedition. Still there was no knowing as to what would come next—how the expedition would terminate, and when the Maharaja would return home. The message from His Highness, therefore, announcing the happy termination of the expedition, and his safe return from the field of battle, brought peace to the anxious minds of the people, and gave life and glee to every hearth and home in the State.

The next day appeared the following telegram in the *Pioneer* of that date :—

"Kung, 28th September.

The troops are now enjoying a well-earned rest. The Somersets left to-day, as did the Maharaja of Patiala. His escort has been employed in reconnoitring under Hira Singh, and has been found most useful. The Patiala Regiment was used under General Graves in chastising the Mitai and Saran Valleys, and came in contact with the enemy. His Highness has been treated like any other soldier, and has shared all the hardships of service. He accepted all these like a true soldier, took the greatest interest in what was going on, and showed the true Sikh keenness to see fighting."

This was the first expression of public opinion about what the Maharaja and the troops of Patiala had done to put a stop to the fire of fanaticism that was running along the whole North-West frontier of India, inflaming the minds of tribe after tribe against the "infidel" Government; and, coming as it did directly from the persons who must have witnessed with their own eyes, or themselves engaged in, the operations, it heightened the joy of the people of Patiala. It added satisfaction to their joy to know that their ruler was not only returning in safety, but with the honor of his house unsullied, the traditions of his ancestors unmarred, the reputation of the Sikh nation untainted. Reaching Peshawar on the 29th of September, His Highness left there the next day for Patiala by special train. General Gaselee, commanding Peshawar district, with other officers of the Peshawar garrison, was present on the platform to say good-bye to His Highness. A guard-of-honor with band and colours was in attendance, and the train left under the usual salute.

The news of His Highness' return from the frontier spread like wild-fire throughout the province, and Sikh gentlemen full of enthusiasm, pleasure and pride, mustered strong at every big station on the line to do honor to the Prince who had so nobly represented the Sikh loyalty and bravery on the battle-field The enthusiasm increased in fervour as the train advanced on its downward journey, and the news had time to penetrate far and wide into the depths of the province, till at last it reached its highest pitch at Ludhiana, the last big station on the route to Patiala. T: demonstration of joy here was simp overwhelming. An immense crowd h: athered there to give a fitting receptio His Highness the Maharaja, and as t train convey- ing His Highness stea: in, people in their eagerness to catch : first glimpse of the hero of the day, climbed up the Maharaja's saloon, showered flowers on him, and with triumphant shouts of " Sat Sri akal " stirred up the emotions of the true disciples of the Guru.

At Patiala the joy of the people knew no bounds. Those were the Dassehra days, and the glorious return of His Highness the Maharaja to Patiala on the 1st of October, 1898, was like Rama's triumphant entry into Ajodhia. On the 5th October, four days later, came off the Dassehra festival itself, and was celebrated with more than usual pomp and *eclat*. Deputations of the several communities of Patiala and others from

outside waited on His Highness the
Maharaja this day, and presented His
Highness with addresses of congratulations on his safe and successful return
home from the frontier.

Great indeed was the enthusiasm
aroused in the minds of the Sikh people
by the part His Highness the Maharaja
had taken in the frontier operations.
And to convey His Highness' thanks to
these people, who had expressed so much
joy at his departure to the frontier and
thanked God for his subsequent safe return to his capital, the following letter
was sent by His Highness the Maharaja,
through his Private Secretary, to the
Khalsa Bahadur of Lahore, which was
supposed to have a wide circulation
among the Sikhs, and through whose
medium it was thought His Highness'
thanks would reach each and all. The
letter runs thus :—

" I am ordered by His Highness the

Maharaja to write this to you, in the hope that you would be kind enough to convey, through the medium of your widely circulated and highly-esteemed paper, the organ of the Sikh nation, His Highness' best thanks to the various Singh bodies and Sikh gentlemen who have been pleased to send messages of congratulations to His Highness on His Highness' safe return home from the frontier. The one uniform sentiment of good-will towards His Highness and loyalty to the British Government, with whose fortunes Providence has thought fit to incorporate the fortunes of the Sikhs, that runs throughout these messages, has deeply impressed His Highness. His Highness knows that it was not as a mere Chief of Patiala, but as the representative of the Khalsa nation—a nation not one whit less in loyalty to the British Throne, not one whit less in devotion to the British cause than the British themselves—that his appearance in the frontier by the side of the English army has evoked the enthusiasm amongst the Sikhs that it *has* evoked. And it was as such that His Highness volunteered his services on the present occasion. For if there is anything which His Highness values above every-thing else, and which he cherishes as the most solemn and sacred trust, it is the loyalty to the British Government that has descended to him from his ancestors, and the good name that the Sikhs have, by their gallant and loyal deeds in the past, secured for themselves; and this loyalty and this good name it is the con-stant care of His Highness and his sin-cere prayer to the Akal Purkh to main-tain. And His Highness hopes and trusts that this is the care and this the prayer of not one, but of every one of the true disciples of the Guru, and that when duty calls,—the duty to take the field against any foe that threatens the stability of the British Empire—the Sikh, true to the instincts of war, and in obedience to the teachings of his religion, no matter wherever and in whatever circumstances he may happen to be, will not fail to respond to it with the enthusiasm and devotion characteristic of his race collectively and individually"

Commenting on this letter, the *Punjab Patriot* of Lahore wrote:—"The letter speaks for itself. His Highness simply voices the genuine feeling which upheaves the breast of every true follower of the Sat Guru when he says: 'if there is anything which His Highness values above all, and which he cherishes as the most solemn and sacred trust, it is the loyalty to the British Government that has descended to him from his ancestors.' The Maharaja who is capable of writing this letter is certainly capable of any achievement in any direction, and the Sikhs are rightly proud of having him as their chief, nor can the British Government wish for a braver and more whole-heartedly devoted friend and feudatory."

CHAPTER IV.

REDUCTION IN THE TIRAH EXPEDITIONARY FORCE AND RETURN OF THE IMPERIAL SERVICE TROOPS.

THE troops still remained on the frontier. The Mohmand Expedition had only dealt with one phase of the frontier operations. The Afridis, who had caught the contagion of fanaticism with the other tribes, had grown the most pestilential of all, and had yet to be dealt with. It had been seen from the first that the troubles on the frontier would not come to an end without a sharp engagement with this tribe. But then the Afridis were known to be highly superior in number and strength to all the other tribes on the border, and it required some time to organize an expedition to be led with success against them. The campaign was organized on a very large scale, and

by the time the Mohmand Expedition
was brought to a close, arrangements
had been made complete for an advance
into the Tirah country. If had been
previously arranged that after the Mohmand Expedition had come to a close,
the services of the forces comprising the
Mohmand Field Force should be utilized
for the Tirah campaign. Thus, while
His Highness the Maharaja left the
country of the Mohmands for Patiala,
the Imperial Service Troops left for
Kohat, *via* Peshawar, where it again
joined the 3rd Column under General
Westmacott to take part in the Tirah
campaign. At Kohat the Patiala Infantry discharged the garrison duties,
and were, besides, posted in the line
of communication. They were told
off to do duties at Garunt Fort, Gomut,
Bhanda, Lachi, Gadu Khel and Bahadur
Khel on the Bannu Road, and they did
whatever was required of them.

But a reduction in the Tirah expeditionary force soon became visible, and on the 15th of January, 1898, His Honor the Lieutenant-Governor of the Punjab, while conveying to His Highness an expression of the Government of India's warmest appreciation of the services of these troops, intimated, by wire, that they will very shortly return to their State. His Highness, however, wished that the troops should see some more fighting, and have some more opportunity of distinguishing themselves in active service. But their services were no longer required, and they returned to Patiala on the 28th of January. From the railway station the troops proceeded straight to the Barodari grounds, and were received there by His Highness the Maharaja in full darbar. Among the British officers of the Imperial Service Troops present on the occasion was Colonel Sir Howard Melliss,

K. C. S. I., occupying a seat on a golden chair to the right of the Maharaja. Great enthusiasm prevailed on the occasion, the smart appearance of the soldiers and officers of the regiment—who, after having nobly maintained the high reputation of the Sikh nation in a trying campaign, had returned to their home, happy and contented---sending a thrill of joy to the hearts of all present there. After the several officers of the regiment had been presented to the Maharaja, His Highness rose and addressed the assembly in an eloquent speech, well suited to the occasion, in Urdu, of which the following is a translation :—

" Sir Howard, Bakshi Bahab, and Officers of the Imperial Service Troops, —Before I have the pleasure to congratulate you all upon the safe and happy return of the Patiala Imperial Service Troops from the frontier, I think it proper to state that the hardships, self-sacrifice and loyalty with which the Patiala Imperial Service Troops have tried to perform the services of the Supreme Government on this occasion have given me infinite joy.

" When you left Patiala for the front. I expressed the hope that you would leave no stone unturned to maintain the name of the Sikhs and the honor of the State by displaying your bravery in the field of battle ; and I am very glad that you have tried your best to carry out my wishes. The honor which the Supreme Government has conferred upon me personally on this occasion, by allowing me and my staff to go to the front, has afforded me the opportunity of seeing some of your services in the field with my own eyes, and I have great pleasure to say that these services of yours have given me satisfaction in every way and, what is more, the British officers also under whose command you have had the honor to serve

in this campaign, have expressed their
satisfaction at your work. In the despatch submitted by him to the Government of India, Major-General Elles has
praised your performances in the Mitai
and Suran Valleys under Lieutenant-
Colonel Graves, and the reconnaissance
work done by the field troop of the Patiala Rajendra Lancers that went with me
as my personal escort. While in his letter
to me of the 3rd October, 1897. Major-
general Elles speaks very highly of your
soldierly conduct and good discipline.
And I believe you will feel still greater
pleasure to hear that His Excellency
the Viceroy and Governor-General of
India has also done me the honor of
conveying to me an expression of Her
Most Gracious Majesty the Queen-Empress of India's appreciation of the services of the State on this occasion

" Gentlemen, although the Supreme
Government has on such occasions before

this honored the troops of the State by
affording them the opportunity of showing
what they can do for the Government,
it is a matter of the greatest pleasure
and pride that this time the troops were
considered fit enough to take their place
in the fighting line side by side with the
experienced and regular troops of the
Supreme Government, to display acts of
gallantry in routing the enemies of the
British Crown. But all this is due to the
earnest efforts of the British officers who
have been deputed by the Supreme
Government to train and discipline you.
And I am glad to take this opportunity
of sincerely thanking these officers, and
especially Colonel Sir Howard Melliss
who have taken a real interest in your
welfare from the beginning.

" I now congratulate you sincerely on
your safe and glorious return home from
the field of battle, and thank the Supreme
Government from the bottom of my heart

for the honor they have conferred on me. I hope, that in future too, whenever such an occasion should present itself the Government of India, while utilising the services of other troops, it will not forget the troops of the Patiala state, and I pray to Akal-Parkh to give us strength to enable us to maintain the reputation gived by our ancestors, by as faithfully serving for the interests of the Government as they did, and to be ever ready at the Service of the Government to whom we owe so much

"Lastly, I now gladly give permission to Bakheshi Saheb to award you the robes of honor and other rewards you so richly deserve."

Colonel Sir Howard Melliss replying spoke as follows :—

"Your Highness.—Permit me to add a few words to the eloquent ones which have just fallen from your lips. On behalf of the British officers who accom-

panied the Patiala Imperial Service
Troops, and of whom you have just
spoken so kindly let me offer you their
grateful thanks. Your Highness' splen-
did regiment standing before us now was
the first of all Imperial Service Regiments to take the field. It was the first
who came under fire and it nobly maintained the high reputation of the Sikh
nation. The men endured the hardships and vicissitudes of a trying campaign in a manner which has commanded
the approbation of all who watched their
progress with interest. I am here to-day
to assure you how much the Government
of India appreciates the good work the
regiment has done, and to congratulate
your Highness and the regiment on your
return home to Patiala."

The robes of honor and other prizes
comprising gold bangles, &c., were now
awarded to the several officers of the
regiment, after which His Highness the

Maharaja and Colonel Sir Howard Melliss with other British Officers of the Imperial Service Troops rose to inspect the regiment, which was drawn up in front of the Darbar pavillion pitched for the occasion, and congratulated the soldiers as they passed down their lines on their safe return from the expedition.

In the afternoon, a gymkhana was held in connection with celebration of the occasion, the most interesting event of which was a tug-of-war between the 1st and the 2nd Battalions of the Imperial Service Infanty. In the evening His Highness the Maharaja gave a dinner, to which about forty gentlemen, including the British officers of the Imperial Service Troops, were invited. After the toast of Her Gracious Majesty the Queen-Empress has been duly honored, Colonel Sir Howard Melliss rose to propose the health of His Highness the Maharaja in the following terms :—

"Your Highness and gentlemen.—
When last I had the honor of drinking
your Highness' health within these walls,
it was on an occasion when I compli-
mented you on the growing efficiency of
your Imperial Service Troops, and you
may recollect telling us at the time that
as you had been first on the polo ground,
and first on the race course, you hoped
that if ever your troops were sent to war
they might be first in the field and that
you would be there to lead them   That,
gentlemen, was sometime ago, and since
then the Patiala troops have been first to
take the field, while you, Maharaja, a
leader of the great Sikh nation, went
forth, amidst the applause and approbation not only of your own subjects but of
the people of India also, to take your
place amongst the soldiers of the Queen-
Empress, and fight against her enemies.

Gentlemen, none of us will forget the
impressive sight we witnessed this morn-

ing when His Highness in Darbar received his gallant regiment on its return from
war, and all of us, I venture to say, did
fully realize how deep is the interest
which His Highness takes in his soldiers.
Later in the day I had the honor of
inspecting the Imperial Service Cavalry,
and I take this opportunity of informing
you, Maharaja, that I found them in a
highly efficient state.

"Your Highness was kind enough this
morning to tell us that we British officers
had done so much to make your troops
efficient, but let me assure you that what
has been accomplished is also greatly due
to the cordial support afforded us by your
state officials, amongst whom I would
mention my old friend, your Commander-
in-chief Sirdar Bahadur Bakhshi Ganda
Sing.

"Gentlemen, I am not going to detain
you by a long after-dinner speech, but in
proposing the health of His Highness I

think I express the wish of all present when I say we hope that he may continue to be first on the polo ground and first on the race course, and should he again join the armies across the frontier, that he will come back as he has now in safety and with honor.

"Gentlemen, long life, health and prosperity to our host, His Highness the Maharaja of Patiala."

His Highness the Maharaja then proposed the health of Colonel Sir Howard Melliss and said :—

"Sir Howard and gentlemen.—I rise to tender you my best thanks for the kind manner in which you have proposed and drunk my health to-night. It is really highly gratifying to me to hear from so high an authority as yourself about the efficiency of my troops, both cavalry and infantry. But as I said this morning, this efficiency has been brought about to a great extent by the earnest

efforts of the British officers themselves
who look after them. Indeed, it is on
account of the training imparted to them
by such kind tutors as yourself, whom I
have known for eight years—and the
other British officers that we see the
troops turned out good pupils to-day.

" Gentlemen, I fully realize the responsibility of my position not only as the
ruler of the Patiala State, but also as the
leader of the Sikh nation. I am proud
that I have been hitherto able, by the
grace of God, to follow in the footsteps
of my forefathers, and I assure you that
whenever there is any danger threatening
the stability of the British Empire, I
shall be the first to come forward not
only with the regiment which has just
been to the war, but with the whole of
my troops to fight for the British cause.
And speaking for the Sikhs I might say
that they, true to the instincts of war
and obedient to the teachings of their

religion, will never be found wanting in
that spirit of loyalty and devotion to the
British crown which has been characteristic of their race collectively and individually.

"Gentlemen, I now propose the health
of Colonel Sir Howard Melliss, who I
hope will not leave us without having
one day's cricket with us."

In the course of its comments on His
Highness the Maharaja's Darbar speech
on this occasion, the *Punjab Patriot* in
its issue of 7th February had the following:—"The Maharaja Patiala, whom his
nation holds in high esteem, is never
happier except when enthusiastically em-
phasising the necessity and desirability of
the Sikhs giving their all to the service of
Her Majesty the Queen Empress. The
Maharaja is proud of the fact that his
ancestors distinguished themselves by
coming to the aid of the British in some
of the critical occasions when the very

existence of the British Power trembled
in the balance. Himself no mean soldier and sportsman, the enlightened ruler
of Patiala is the living embodiment of
an active young chief, whose whole-heart-
ed loyalty is quite as intense as his zest
for sport."

CHAPTER V.

THIS was the first time in the history
of Patiala that the Imperial Service
Troops ever saw active service, and this
was the first time in the history of India
that a ruling Prince ever proceeded in
person to the scene of war to fight in defence of Her Majesty's empire in India.
And the manner in which both the
Maharaja and the troops behaved themselves on this occasion under fire, excited
the admiration of all who witnessed or
watched the rough game of war. Nor
were the Government and its officers
slow to appreciate the dash, gallantry
and discipline displayed by the Maharaja and the troops throughout the expedition. In relinquishing command of
the Mohmand Field Force, Major-General
Elles wrote in a Field Force Order

No. 155 Special, dated Camp Melmiana, 5th October, 1897 :—"It has not been the fortune of the force to see much fighting, but on several occasions parts of the division have been engaged with the enemy, and though resistance was small, heavy work has been entailed on the troops. . . . . It has been a great satisfaction to General Elles to have under his command the 1st Patiala Regiment and the Nabha Infantry of the Imperial Service Troops. The former regiment has taken its place in the fighting line with the regular troops, and both regiments have done good work " While in a private letter to His Highness the Maharaja, Major-General Elles writes :—" It gives me much pleasure to inform you that I have had a letter from General Graves bringing to notice the good work done by the Patiala cavalry and infantry on the 25th September, when carrying out the punishment. of the Suran Valley. The

Patiala infantry came under the fire of the enemy whilst covering the retirement. Your cavalry has on several occasions done very useful reconnaissance work and have more than once come under fire.

I shall have much pleasure in bringing the services of your Highness' troops to the notice of the Government of India in due course. I have had the Patiala infantry with me for the last four days and have had an opportunity of noticing their soldierly conduct and good discipline. I hope you had a pleasant journey back to Patiala and were not delayed on the way, and that your health has in no way suffered by the hard work you have undergone." " I am very much gratified," wrote back the Maharaja in reply, " to hear from you that my troops, both cavalry and infantry, have acquitted themselves to the satisfaction of the officers under whom they had the honor of being led against the enemy. The Patiala troops, you

know, had their baptism of fire in the
Mohmand Expedition, and the manner
in which they have, at this time, behaved
under fire, reflects credit not upon the
troops so much as upon the British
officers themselves, under whose training
and discipline they have been, or under
whose leadership they had the good
fortune of advancing up against the foe.
And I am glad to take this opportunity
of giving expression to my feelings of
thankfulness to the Government and its
officers for the interest they have ever
evinced in my troops, and for the honor
they have now conferred on them by ac-
cepting the offer of their services
on the present occasion. As for myself,
I have only to thank yourself for the
kindness you showed me all along. In
fact it was this kindness of yours that
made so very light to me the work which
would otherwise have been somewhat
hard indeed. But hard or light, I am

ever ready at the service of the British
Government with cheerfulness of heart,
and with the true feelings of loyalty that
I have the pride of having inherited from
my forefathers."

What His Excellency the Viceroy and
Governor-General of India thought of the
loyalty which prompted His Highness to
volunteer his services, of the promptitude
with which His Highness started for the
frontier, and of the part which His Highness took in the operations there, is best
shown by the following letter which His
Excellency was pleased to write to His
Highness from Simla on November 4th,
1897, after His Highness had returned
from the frontier. "I have had it in my
mind," so wrote His Excellency, "to
write a few lines to convey to you an
expression of the gratification which your
action in connection with the frontier
troubles has given me. Your departure
was so prompt that I had then no oppor-

tunity, but I hope you will consider it no
less appropriate now when I can congratulate you on the part that you have
taken. I can share the satisfaction of
the people of your State at seeing their
Chief prepared to emulate the manly
deeds of his ancestors.

I have been specially directed by
Her Majesty the Queen-Empress to
make known to the Princes of India
her sense of the loyalty and devotion
which have inspired their offers of
assistance and of personal service. It
gives me as much pleasure to be the medium for forwarding to Your Highness, as
I am sure it will give Your Highness to
receive, this message of Her Majesty's
approval." " It is a letter," wrote His
Highness in acknowledgment of, and in
reply to, His Excellency's letter, " of
which I may well feel proud ; containing,
as it does, an expression of Your Excellency's satisfaction at, and of Her Most

Gracious Majesty's approval of, what it has been my great pleasure to do in placing my own personal services, and those of my troops, at the disposal of the State in connection with the frontier troubles, which I rejoice to believe are now nearly at an end. In doing so I have been actuated by those feelings of truest loyalty and devotion to Her Most Gracious Majesty the Queen-Empress which have ever guided the actions of my forefathers : and Your Excellency will be adding to the many proofs of your kindness towards me if you will be pleased to convey to Her Majesty the assurance that the present ruler of the Patiala State will never be found less eager than those forefathers to testify to his devoted loyalty to Her throne, and to his profound reverence for Her gracious person."

The formal despatch of Major-General Elles on the Mohmand Expedition appeared in the *Pioneer* of the 7th Decem-

ber, and after enumerating the main
difficulties to contend with, which were
the passes over which roads had always
to be made and anxiety regarding water,
as in the western Mohmand country, the
supply being almost entirely from tanks
the dams of which had been cut by the,
Mohmands, and which often only contained a little dirty water, closed with the following remarks :—" The Imperial Service
Troops under my command proved their
fitness to fight in the first line, and were
utilized exactly the same as regular
troops. The cavalry escorts of the Patiala and Jodhpore cavalry did good
reconnaissance work on more than one
occasion and came under fire. The First
Patiala Regiment was employed under
Lt.-Col. Graves in the operations in
the Mitai and Suran Valleys, and covered
the retirement of the brigade under
fire ; their good service was brought to
my notice by the General Officer Com-

manding the 3rd Brigade. The Nabha
Regiment, owing to its having been added
to my force late in September, had to be
kept on the line of communications." In
conclusion Major-General Elles acknow-
ledges the hearty co-operation of his staff,
and returns his best thanks, amongst
others, to His Highness the Maharaja,
who "has most cheerfully borne all
hardships and took the greatest interest
in the operations."

The despatch was preceded by a letter
from the Adjutant-General, which contained the following :—His Excellency
(the Commander-in-Chief) has read with
very great satisfaction the complimen-
tary terms in which General Elles has
alluded to the work done by the Imperial
Service Troops, and he is confident
that the Government of India will cordi-
ally endorse what is said in the despatch, not only as regards them, but also
as regards the services of the two native

Princes who shared with their British and native comrades the dangers and hardships of the campaign.

The Governor-General in Council concurs in the above opinion, and expresses approbation of the excellent work done by the Imperial Service Troops, and the services rendered by the Maharaja of Patiala and Sir Partap Singh.

The Right Hon'ble the Secretary of State for India, in a Despatch No. 53 Military, dated India Office, London, the 26th May, 1898, to His Excellency the Right Hon'ble the Governor-General of India in Council, published for general information in the *Gazette of India* of June 18th, acknowledged the services of the Patiala State on this occasion in the following words :—

" Her Majesty's Government have noticed with much satisfaction the excellent services of the Imperial Service Troops, who have fought side by side with

Her Majesty's army in this campaign,
and taken their full share of its hardships. Their acknowledgments are due
to the Chiefs of the Native States
who placed their regiments and transport trains at your disposal, and also
to the native Princes, His Highness the Maharaja of Patiala, Major
the Maharaj Rana of Dholpore, Lieute-
nant-Colonel the Maharaja of Cooch-
Behar, G.C.I.E., and Lieutenant-
Colonel Maharaja Dhiraj Sir Partap
Singh, G.C.S.I., of Jodhpur, for their
personal services on the staff in the
field."

The same despatch conveyed the
Secretary of State for India's sanction of
the Viceroy's recommendation that the
India medal with clasp inscribed " Punjab
Frontier, 1897-98," should be conferred
on all the troops (including, of course,
the Imperial Service Troops) in the field,
and the same *Gazette* contained an

announcement that the Governor-General in Council was pleased to sanction the promotion in, and admission to, the Order of British India, 2nd Class, with the title of " Bahadur," of Sardar Sunder Singh, Commandant, 1st Regiment, Patiala Infantry.

———————

CHAPTER VI.

THE STAR OF INDIA.

It was the evening of the 20th of May 1898,—the evening of that memorable day which will ever be regarded as a red-letter day in the annals of the Patiala State. A cricket match—Patiala *versus* Simla—had just finished in Annandale, the sun had just gone down, and His Highness the Maharaja and party had just returned home, when up came a chaprassi from the Government House bringing a letter for His Highness the Maharaja. It was the eve of Her Majesty's birthday, and the appearance of the man with a letter from the Government House at such an hour on such a day naturally enlivened the minds of all those present with a lively sense of the honors to come. And, oh! joy, the letter when opened proved a letter from His Excellency Lord Elgin, Viceroy and Governor-General of India, bringing the welcome news that His Highness had been appointed as G.C.S.I. "I have much pleasure in informing you," wrote His Excellency, "that Her Majesty has approved of your appointment as G. C. S. I., and that it will be announced in the Gazette to-morrow; and I offer my very sincere congratulations to Your Highness, and if I may say so, to the gallant Sikh nation of which you are an acknowledged representative, on this signal mark of Her Majesty's appreciation of your and their devotion and loyalty.

"Perhaps Your Highness will permit me to add an expression of my earnest hope and expectation that the honor thus conferred will be a fresh stimulus to your endeavour to perform the duties of your high station. Your Highness has long excelled in manly exercises, and last year showed your readiness to engage in the rough game of war in defence of the interests of the Empire.

That it may also ever be your aim to promote the best interests of your people and to secure for the inhabitants of your State the peace and contentment which Her Majesty desires for all her subjects is a wish which I trust you will not decline to accept from

> Your sincere friend,
>
> (Sd.) LORD ELGIN."

The letter in itself, written in His Excellency's own hand-writing, and couched in the friendliest of terms, was an honor to His Highness. And then the message it conveyed. It simply overwhelmed His Highness and all who learnt it, with feelings of joy and gratitude. The Maharaja was glad and proud that he had been appointed as G. C. S. I. He was glad and proud that he had gained what his ancestors were proud to enjoy, and he was glad and proud that what little he had been able to do in defence of the interests of the Empire, had been appreciated by Her Majesty's Government. And the letter His Highness wrote in reply to His Excellency is characteristic of him. "It is with a proud pleasure," he wrote, "and a grateful heart that I write this to tender my most sincere thanks to your Excellency for the very kind letter in which Your Excellency has been pleased to convey to me Her Most Gracious Majesty's approval of my appointment as G. C. S. I. This fresh and signal mark of Her Majesty's appreciation of the devotion and loyalty to the British throne, which feelings I have the pride of having inherited from my forefathers, is another proof that the Queen Empress, with a mother's kind heart, is never unmindful of the services rendered to her Government at any time by the dutiful sons of the British Empire, and will, I am sure, be hailed with delight as a tribute to the

Sikh bravery and loyalty by the entire Sikh nation I am proud to represent.

" I am fully alive to the new responsibilities that attach themselves to me as the recipient of the high honor thus conferred on me. I assure Your Excellency that next to the loyalty and devotion to the person and throne of Her Most Gracious Majesty, nothing will be nearer and dearer to my heart than the welfare of my people.

" Again thanking your Excellency, and requesting you to kindly convey this assurance of mine, together with my loyal homage and my heartfelt thanks, to Her Majesty for the gracious kindness with which Her Majesty has been pleased to confer on me the same high honor which my ancestors were proud to enjoy.

I remain,

Your Excellency's very sincere friend,

(Sd.)　RAJINDRA SINGH,

Maharaja Patiala."

Next day, the 21st of May, appeared
the *Gazette of India* containing a Notifi-
cation, dated Simla, the 21st May, 1898,
No. 46 S. I., in which His Excellency the Grand Master of the Most
Exalted Order of the Star of India was
pleased to announce that Her Majesty
the Queen, Empress of India, had been
graciously pleased to make the following
appointment to the said Order : To be a
Knight Grand Commander His Highness Fazand-i-Khas-i-Daulat-i Inglishia,
Mansur-i-Zaman, Amir-ul-Umra Maharaja Dhiraj Rajeshwar, Sri Maharaja-
Rajgan Rajindra Singh Mahindra Bahadur, of Patiala.

This announcement was universally
received with satisfaction in Simla, and
on the 29th May deputations of the
Sikh, Hindu, Mahomedan and Parsee
communities of that place waited upon
His Highness the Maharaja and presented him with addresses of congratula-

tions, His Highness the Kanwar Saheb of Patiala and Prince Ranjitsinghji being also present.

Replying to the addresses, His Highness the Maharaja said :—

"Your Highnesses and Gentlemen, please allow me to thank you all for the sincerity with which you have been pleased to present me with these addresses congratulating me on the high honor which Her Majesty the Queen-Empress has been graciously pleased to confer on me. It is very kind of you to speak so nicely of my services, but I feel that I have not had enough occasion yet to do my heartfelt desire in serving Her Gracious Majesty the Queen-Empress and my country as I should like. But I pray to Akalpurukh that I may be afforded that pleasure later on. In having offered my own personal services to the Government in connection with the troubles on the frontier, I have done nothing extraordinary. I have only followed in the footsteps of my fore-fathers, for I was inspired by no other motives than devotion and loyalty to the British throne, which sentiments I am proud to say have descended to me from my ancestors. I am indeed thankful to the Supreme Government that they accepted my offer and afforded to me the pleasure of being in active service. Gentlemen, we are very fortunate that we are living under the benign sway of Her Most Gracious Majesty the Queen Empress and her just and appreciating Government, whose sole aim is to promote the best interests of the Empire; and it is the duty of us all to do whatever we can to help the Government by our hearty and loyal co-operation in the work before it."

It would not be out of place here to give a brief description of the Order of the Star of India. This Most Exalted

Order was instituted by Her Majesty Queen Victoria, 23rd February, 1861, and enlarged 28th March, 1866, and again in 1875 and 1876. It consists of the Sovereign, the Grand Master, and 246 Ordinary Members, together with such extra and Honorary Members as Her Majesty, Her Heirs and Successors, shall from time to time appoint. The 246 Ordinary Members are divided into three classes. The first class are styled Knigths Grand Commanders, and consist of thirty members (eighteen Natives and twelve Europeans) ; the second class of seventy-two members, styled Knights Commanders ; the third class of one hundred and forty-four members, styled Companions. Her Most Gracious Majesty the Queen and Empress of India is the Sovereign, and His Excellency the Viceroy and Governor-General of India is the Grand Master and first Principal Knight ; of the Order.

The Statutes enable the Sovereign
to confer the dignity of Knight Grand
Commander of the Order upon such
Princes and Chiefs of India as shall have
entitled themselves to Her Majesty's
favour; and upon such of Her Majesty's
British subjects as have, by important
and loyal services rendered by them to
the Indian Empire, merited the Royal
favour; and the second and the third
classes upon persons who, by their conduct or services in the Indian Empire,
have merited the Royal favour. The
Insignia of the Order consist of a Star,
a Badge, a Collar, and a Mantle.

The Badge is an onyx cameo of Her Majesty's effigy, set in a gold and ornamented oval, enamelled in light blue, inscribed with the motto of the Order "Heaven's Light our Guide" in diamonds, surmounted by a Star of five points in silver. The riband of the Order is light blue, having a narrow white stripe towards either edge, and is worn from the right shoulder to the left side.

The Collar is composed of the lotus of India, of palm branches, in saltire, tied together by a riband, and of the united Red and White Rose in the centre of the Imperial Crown. All richly enamelled on gold, in their proper colours and linked together by chains of gold to the said Crown.

The Star is composed of rays of gold issuing from a centre, having thereon a Star in diamonds, resting upon a light blue enamelled circular riband, tied at the ends, inscribed with the motto of the

Order, *viz.*, "Heaven's Light our Guide,' also in diamonds.

The Mantle—light blue satin. lined with white silk, and fastened with a cordon of white silk, having blue and silver tassels attached thereto, and a representation of the Star of the Order on the left side.

It will be interesting to the readers to learn that His Highness the Maharaja's grandfather, the late Maharaja Narindra Singh, Mahindra Bahadur, was one of the first Knight Grand Commanders of the Order, having been appointed to this Order in the year 1861, the very year in which the Order was instituted.

CHAPTER VII.

HIS EXCELLENCY THE VICEROY'S VISIT TO PATIALA AND INVESTITURE OF HIS HIGHNESS THE MAHARAJA.

It was an occasion of great rejoicing in Patiala. His Excellency the Viceroy and Governor-General of India was coming to the Capital of the State to invest His Highness the Maharaja with the insignia of the Most Exalted Order of the Star of India. As a rule Chapters for investiture are held at Viceregal Headquarters at Calcutta, and it was as an act of special favour and high honor, of which the Maharaja and the State felt justly proud, that His Excellency the Viceroy thought fit to hold the Investiture Durbar at Patiala, and having regard to the services of the Patiala State and the high honor it has ever enjoyed at the hands of the British Government it was quite in the fitness of things that it

should have been so. " I think," said
His Excellency the Viceroy in the course
of his speech after the Investiture, " it
will be recognized that under any circumstances this was fitting, but if so, it
was abundantly fitting in the circumstances of the times in which we live."

Most extensive preparations were
made by the Durbar for the reception
of His Excellency the Viceroy and Governor-General of India. Arrangements
for His Excellency's accommodation
were made in that pretty little garden
called Moti Bagh, while in front of the
Bagh was laid a beautiful Camp for His
Honor the Lieutenant-Governor who was
to be present on this occasion. " The
hospitality of Patiala which is always
lavish," wrote a correspondent to a Bombay paper, "assumed a right royal character on this special occasion."

His Honor the Lieutenant-Governor
had already arrived in the Camp at 7 in

the morning. His Excellency the Viceroy was timed to arrive at 1-30 P.M., and
a few minutes before the appointed time
His Honor the Lieutenant-Governor,
His Highness the Maharaja accompanied by His Highness the Kanwar
Saheb, Prince Ranjitsinghji and high
officials of the State, Sir Howard Melliss,
K.C.S I., Lord Frederick Blackwood,
Herr Von Waldthausen, the German
Consul-General,—the last three had
arrived by a special train the day before,—
proceeded to the Railway station to receive His Excellency. The station presented a handsome spectacle with its
decorations of bunting festoons and
flowers,—decorations which were greatly
enhanced by the briiliant assembly that
awaited the train, the guard of honor with
band and colours that was drawn up there,
and the long line of cavalry and gorgeously
caparisoned horses and elephants that
stretched along the road leading from

the platform. Punctually at 1-30 P.M., the Viceregal train steamed in, and as His Excellency the Viceroy alighted from the train, the guard of Honor presented arms, the bugles sounded, and a battery of horse artillery stationed outside thundered forth a loyal salute of 31 guns. His Excellency was received by His Highness the Maharaja on the platform, and was conducted by him to His Highness' celebrated gold and silver carriage that waited outside. A procession was now formed and His Excellency drove with His Highness by the Mall Road to the Moti Bagh.

The roads gay with bunting and Venetian masts, were lined with troops, and dense crowds collected at various points; most picturesque crowds, too, with their immense Sikh lungies of beautiful pale colours of many shades. As the procession approached Moti Bagh it passed through the serried lines of the

Imperial Service Troops, a truly fine body of soldiers. On arriving at the Moti Bagh it was delightful to pass through the gateway out of the heat and glare of the sun into the shade of the green and beautiful garden which, carpeted with green turf, and with fountains springing up sparkling in the sun, could not but recall fairy visions of the "Arabian Nights" stories. The Maharaja paid his ceremonial visit to the Viceroy and then left for the Palace. After luncheon the Viceroy granted an interview to Hon'ble Baba Sir Khem Singh Bedi, while Lady Elgin, accompained by Lady Young, Colonels Owen and Franklin, visited the Hospitals in which His Highness takes so much interest.

At 6 P.M. the Viceroy had to pay his return visit to the Palace, which was also the opportunity chosen to invest the Maharaja with the Grand Cross of the Star of India. The deputation consisting of His Highness the Kour Sahib and the four principal Sirdars of the Patiala State which was to wait on the Grand Master at the Viceregal Camp at 5-40 P.M. precisely to conduct His Excellency to the Maharaja's Palace was dispensed with by His Excellency. The Viceroy started from the Camp at 5-50 P.M. accompanied by His Honor the Lieutenant-Governor of the Punjab, and attended by the Secretary of the Order, the Private and Military Secretaries, and His Excellency's personal staff.

Dusk was falling when His Excellency started for the Palace escorted by Lancers driving with the Lieutenant-Governor. As the carriage neared the Palace, the illuminations, at first faint in the dying light, began to twinkle and then to burn till a fairyland seemed to hang between earth and sky in the Palace of the sombre and somewhat gloomy Punjab

City. As the carriages turned into the Palace Courtyard amid the crash of drums and the blare of trumpets the sight afforded was really striking. Torches flaring among the crowd showed the eager sea of faces, the horses of the Lancers snorting and stamping, the glimmering lance points, and the dark background of the high walls and casements of the buildings crowned and crowded with dark faces and glistening eyes. The Maharaja met His Excellency at the foot of the red carpeted stairs and a procession was formed passing through ranks of scarlet and gold retainers to the robing room, where the Viceroy as Grand Master, and Sir W. Cunningham as Secretary, donned their robes of the Order.

While His Excellency the Viceroy was conducted to the Robing Room, His Honor the Lieutenant-Governor, was conducted by His Highness the Maha-

raja to his seat in the Durbar Hall.
His Honor the Lieutenant-Governor,
His Highness the Maharaja of Patiala
and the guests being seated, His Excellency the Grand Master and his suite
entered the Durbar Hall in the following
Order:—The Secretary of the order,
wearing the mantle and the badge of
the order, aide-de-camp to the Viceroy,
Military Secretary to the Viceroy, aide-
de-camp to the Viceroy, Private Secretary
to the Viceroy, His Excellency the
Grand Master, wearing the robe and insignia of the order, attendants of H. E.
the Grand Master.

The Band played the National Anthem
and the guard of Honor presented arms.

H. H. the Maharaja sat on the right of
His Excellency, while on the right of the
Maharaja sat the Political officer on
duty with His Highness and beyond him
were Kour Ranbir Singh and the Sirdars
in immediate attendance on His Highness,

not exceeding nine in number, according to their rank. His Honor the Lieutenant-Governor of the Punjab was accommodated with a seat on the *dais* on the left of His Excellency. On the left of the Lieutenant-Governor the Secretary of the Order, the Private and Military Secretaries and His Excellency's personal Staff were seated. The Sirdars| and officials of the state were seated behind the nine Sirdars in attendance on the Maharaja, the inivited guests being seated behind His Excellency's Staff.

All present rose and remained standing until His Excellency had taken his seat on the *dais*. The superb lighting of the great Hall, the blaze of jewels, the flashing of colours, the clank of swords, the rustle of silks when the assembly rose and sat again, was quite dazzling. After all had resumed their seats, the Secretary of the Order reported that the business before the assembly was the investiture,

under the Sovereign's grant, of His Highness the Maharaja Rajindra Singh of
Patiala as a Knight Grand Commander,
and the decoration, under, a similar grant
of LucasWhite King, Esq., of the Indian
Civil Service, as a Companion of the
Most Exalted Order of the Star of India.

His Excellency thereupon commanded
the Secretary to read the Sovereign's
grant of the dignity of Knight Grand
Commander, which read as follows:—

*"Victoria, by the Grace of God, of the
United Kingdom of Great Britain and
Ireland, Queen, Defender of the Faith,
Empress of India, and Sovereign of the
Most Exalted Order of the Star of
India. To His Highness the Maharaja of Patiala, Greeting, Whereas
We are desirous of conferring upon
you such a mark of Our Royal favour
as will evince the esteem in which We
hold your person and the services which
you have rendered to Our Indian Empire, We have thought fit to nominate
and appoint You to be a Knight Grand*

Commander of Our said Most Exalted Order of the Star of India. We do by these Presents grant unto you the dignity of a Knight Grand Commander of Our said Order, and hereby authorise you to have, hold and enjoy the said dignity and rank as a Knight Grand Commander of Our aforesaid Order, together with all and singular the privileges thereunto belonging or appertaining.

Given at Our Court at Balmoral under Our Sign Manual and the Seal of Our said Order, this twenty-first day of May, 1898, in the sixty-first year of Our Reign.

By the Sovereign's Command,

(Sd) George Hamilton.

Grant of the dignity of Knight Grand Commander of the Order of the Star of India to His Highness the Maharaja of Patiala.

All present with the exception of the Grand Master and Lieutenant-Governor rose when the grant was commanded to be read, and remained standing until the proclamation hereinafter mentioned was made.

After the grant was read, the Secretary of the Order conducted the Maharaja to the presence of the Grand Master, to whom His Highness made his reverence, and then to the table (placed on the left of His Excellency and on the right of the line of chairs for His Excellency's suite) on which the Insignia had been laid, and there decorated His Highness successively with the Riband, Badge and Star, and robed him with the Mantle, of the Order. This done, the Maharaja was conducted by the Secretary to the front of the *dais*, and made his reverence to the Grand Master. The Secretary took from the table the Collar of a Knight Grand Commander and with due reverence delivered it to the Grand Master.

The Grand Master, remaining seated, then invested the Maharaja with the

Collar, and addressed to him the following admonition :—

" In the name of the Queen, Empress of India, and by Her Majesty's Command, I hereby invest you with the Honorable Insignia of the Order of the Star of India, of which Most Exalted Order Her Majesty has been graciously pleased to appoint you to be a Knight Grand Commander."

When the admonition had been given the newly invested Knight Grand Commander made his reverence to the Grand Master and was conducted by the Secretary to his seat at His Excellency's right hand in front of which he remained standing.

The Guard of Honour presented arms, and the Secretary of the Order proclaimed the full titles of the Maharaja, that is to say :—

" His Highness Farzand-i-Khás-i-Daulat-i-Inglishia,   Mansur-i-Zamán,

Amir-ul-Umara, Maharaja-Dhiráj Rájesh-
war, Sri Máháraja-i-Rajágán, Sir Rájin-
drá Singh, Mahindra Báhádur, Máhá-
ràja of Patiala, Knight Grand Commander of the Most Exalted Order of
the Star of India."

The proclamation ended, all resumed
their seats, and His Excellency briefly
congratulated the newly invested Knight
Grand Commander.

The Secretary then presented to the
Grand Master the Badge of the Third
Class of the Order for the Companion
to be decorated, and conducted Mr.
Lucas White King to the front of the
dais, where he made his reverence to the
Grand Master.   The Secretary announced Mr. King's name as he was presented
before the Grand Master.

The Grand Master handed the Badge
to the Secretary who attached it in the
proper place.   Thereafter Mr. King
made his reverence to the Grand Master,

and was conducted by the Secretary to his seat.

After the impressive ceremonial of investing the Maharaja and Mr. King had been performed, the Viceroy—who had the Maharaja on his right, in his new pale blue shimmering robes, and scintillating diamonds in his necklace and all around his lungi, a truly regal figure—remained seated and addressed the Durbar. His Excellency said '—" Maharaja, it has been a genuine pleasure to me to come here on this occasion and to invest your Highness with the insignia of of the Exalted Order, to which Her Majesty has been pleased to appoint you, in the capital of your State, and in presence of so many representatives of the Sikh nation. I think it will be recognised that under any circumstances this was fitting, but if so, it was abundantly fitting in the circumstances of the times in which we live. It would be

no great strain on the imagination for us
to fancy that we still heard the echoes
of the strife of last year, and the tramp
of the battalions which Your Highness
and the Rajah of Nabah and other Chiefs
sent out to do battle shoulder to shoulder
with the armies of the Queen-Empress;
and the page lies open before us on
which is inscribed the name of Saragarhi,
that last on the everlengthening list of
deeds of arms which testify to the unflinching bravery and devotion of the
Sikh soldiers I welcome this occasion as
giving me an opportunity of publicly
declaring! the admiration with which
in common with all my countrymen I
regard the constancy and loyalty of the
Sikh Nation. Nor do I think it out of
place to remind you that, mingling with
the echoes to which I have referred,
we find now the softer tone of peace, and
that the proceedings of the *Jirgaks* assembled at Peshawar give good hope th

there will be no further discordant note.
No well-wisher of his country could
desire it to be otherwise. We have
no abiding quarrel, we can desire no
abiding quarrel, with our neighbours in
the hills. On the contrary the policy we
have proclaimed is, I think, the same
which I myself declared at Lahore in
1894 before the assembled chiefs of the
Punjab when I said it was our aim to
leave them the entire occupation of their
country, the fullest measure of autonomy
and the most complete liberty in their
internal affairs to follow their tribal customs. Whatever else may have happened, to this declaration I claim that I have
adhered. No tribe or section of a tribe
has since then been compelled against its
will to surrender any territory or any
right of Self-Government which it desired
to retain. Is there not then some road
to an understanding? The road we
have followed has not been the one which

I would have selected had I been free to choose ; but at the end of it we at any rate know more of the tribes, and they know more of us than was the case before. They on their side know that even in the hour of victory our terms are not cruel or vindictive, and aim at nothing more than a fair and reasonable settlement ; we on our side recognise the soldierly qualities which they have displayed. I cannot deny myself the hope that the time will come when these tribes will prove themselves staunch allies and supporters of British rule in India, and seek to emulate, if they cannot surpass, the reputation in that respect which is the undying heritage of the Sikh Nation.   To Your Highness, as one who by the equipment and maintenance of the Imperial Service Troops and by leading them to the field, has worthily sustained the credit for loyalty of the State and Chief of Patiala. I offer my personal congratulations on the honor

bestowed upon you by Her Majesty. I
desire to congratulate you also Mr. King,
who have known well how to guide and influence the wayward inclinations of the
tribesmen in the right direction, on the
mark of your Sovereign's appreciation,
which I have had the pleasure to convey
to you."

A procession was then formed, which
left the Durbar Hall and marched
to the Robing Room in the following
order :—

The Secretary of the Order, Aide-de-
Camp to the Viceroy. The Military
Secretary to the Viceroy, Aide-de-Camp
to the Viceroy, the Private Secretary to
the Viceroy, His Excellency the Grand
Master. Attendants of His Excellency
the Grand Master, His Highness Maharaja Sir Rajendra Singh Mahindra
Bahadur, G.C.S.I., Mr. King, attendants
of the Maharaja.

A Grand March was performed by the

Band, and the Guard of Honor presented arms.

After the Grand Master and the Knight Grand Commander had divested themselves of their robes and insignia, His Excellency and His Honour the Lieutenant Governor were conducted by the Maharaja to a balcony on the top of the Palace overlooking a large square in front of the Palace Gate. Here a display of fireworks took place, after viewing which Their Excellencies and party drove back to the Moti Bagh. The Maharaja's troops lining the street in the front of the Palace and saluting as His Excellency passed.

At 8 P.M. His Excellency the Viceroy was entertained to a dinner at Moti Bagh,—the party including their Excellencies the Viceroy and the Countess of Elgin, Mr. Babington and Lady Elizabeth Smith, their Highnesses the Maharaja and the Kour Sahib of Patiala and Prince Ranjitsinghji, Sir William Mackwork

Young, K.C.S.I., Lieutenant-Governor of the Punjab and Lady Young, Sir Howard Melliss, K.C.S.I., Lord Blackwood, Baron Waldthausen, Major Angelo, Dr. Owen, C.M.G., C.I.E., and Mrs. Owen, Mr. Dane, Col. Brackenbury, Colonel Durand, Dr. Franklin, Captains Pollen, Adam and Annesley, Aides-de-Camp; Sir William Cunningham, K.C.S.I., Mr. L. W. King, C.S.I., and Mrs. King, Mr. Egerton and Messrs. Barron and Wilson, Civil Service. After the loyal toast had been duly honored, His Highness the Maharaja rose to propose the health of the guest of the evening, His Excellency Lord Elgin, Viceroy and Governor-General of India. His Highness thanked His Excellency for the honor conferred on him that night, and bidding His Excellency good-bye wished him a pleasant voyage home and long and happy life there.

The Viceroy, in replying, said :—

" Your Highness, ladies and gentlemen,

I have already this afternoon expressed
the gratification which it has given me to
attend here to-day to invest the Maharaja with the insignia of the Order, which
Her Majesty has conferred upon him,
and, as he has said, I have endeavoured
to point out that the honor is one which is
done to the Sikh nation of which he is a
representative.   We all, I know, honor
and respect the Sikh nation for the manner in which it has stood by us, in many
difficult times (applause) and we are glad
to see the Chief of Patiala putting
himself once more in the forefront and
leading his men in a time of emergency
(applause). We, I think, all recognise,
that the present Maharaja of Patiala is
a man with much energy, and I at any
rate have nothing to complain of if it
finds an outlet in those manly sports
which we, coming from Britain, value as
a good means of education (applause).
The only thing that I would like to say—

and perhaps the Maharaja will allow me
to claim the privileges of an old friend, as
I have now known him for some years—
is that I should wish those manly sports
and the energy which he puts into
them, would lead on to other things
also. I cannot help thinking that a man
who can make fifty runs against good
bowling has nerve (applause) and I
believe that the man who goes into the
unknown region, as it was then, of the
Mohmand country has pluck (applause).
The two together show resolution, and I
should like my esteemed friend Maharaja to shake off a little of the modesty
which he once or twice expressed to me.
He has told me that, after all, the work
of a statesman or practical administrator
is beyond his capacity. I do not believe
it (hear, hear, and applause,) and I hope
that though we are going away and shall
soon be very far distant from Patiala,
the time will come when we shall

hear that the Maharaja has put himself in the forefront in that capacity also, to the honor of Patiala and the states of the Punjab (applause). I am very sorry, indeed, Maharaja, that time has not permitted us to pay you a longer visit, as you have so hospitably expressed the wish that we should have done. The fact is that it is rather difficult for a Viceroy to make his plans. Even last week the fear came upon me that, with a fate like that which befell me last year, I might be obliged once more to postpone all my journeys. Fortunately the cloud which hung over European politics has lifted a little, and we are able to set forth on our journey. But all I can say is that I am exceedingly glad that I do not leave India without paying even this short visit to the Phulkian States, and I ask you now, ladies and gentlemen to join with me in drinking to the health of the Maharaja of Patiala and prosperity to the Phulkian States of the Punjab.

After dinner His Excellency the Viceroy and suite accompanied by His Honor the Lieutenant-Governor and His Highness the Maharaja drove to the Railway Station and left Patiala by special train at 10 P.M. The departure was private.

His Honor the Lieutenant-Governor stopped for next day at Patiala to present Colonel Sunder Singh of the 1st Patiala Regiment the 2nd class of the order of the British India. A Parade of the Patiala Imperial Service Troops was held the next morning for this purpose. The troops on Parade where the Rajindra Lancers and the First and Second Battalion of the Patiala Infantry. His Highness the Maharaja and His Highness the Kour Saheb with numerous State and Military Officers and Major Angelo and Captain Davidson, Imperial

Service Inspecting Officers were present. The Lieutenant-Governor being accompanied by his Secretaries and Captain Annesley, Aide-de-Camp. The parade took place at 8 o'clock and about two thousand rank-and-file were on parade, the troops presenting a fine soldier-like appearance and being smart and workman-like as well. The Cavalry were on the right of the line with the First Battalion next, and the Second Battalion on the left. The troops, led by the Lancers, marched past in review order, and afterwards the Lancers went by at the trot and then at the Gallop, acquitting themselves in both movements extremely well.

The Infantry marched past very steadily and were a fine compact body of troops. After the march past the "officer's call" was sounded, and the several officers of the Lancers and Infantry marched to the saluting base where H. H. the Lieutenant-Governor

and H H. the Maharaja waited them,
attended by their respective staffs.

Colonel Sunder Singh was called to the
front, and H. H. the Lieutenant-Governor addressed the following speech to
him and the officers present " Maharaja
and Officers of the Imperial Service
Troops of Patiala, –I have been very
glad to see you on parade this morning
and to know that the Imperial Service
Troops of this State are in a state of
high efficiency, and that in regard to
equipment, discipline, and conduct
generally, they are a sample of what
well drilled troops ought to be.

" In conferring upon His Highness
the Maharaja, yesterday, the distinction
which has been given to him by Her
Gracious Majesty the Queen, His
Excellency the Viceroy alluded to the
fact that the Services of the Patiala
State in connection with the recent disturbances has influenced the choice of

Her Majesty in conferring that honor, and I am very glad to be able to say that from all that I have heard of the conduct and behavior of that portion of the Imperial Service Troops of Patiala which went to the front, they have been excellent. I now have the pleasure of conferring upon Colonel Sunder Singh, who commanded that regiment which went on the Mohmand and Tirah expeditions, the Second Class Order of British India in recogniton of he services rendered by the Patiala Imperial Service Troops."

His Honor then left with His Highness the Maharaja and visited the Rajindra Hospital, the Mohendra College and the Jubilee Library, and expressed his pleasure with all he saw.

At eleven o'clock His Honor the Lieutenant Governor paid a return visit to His Highness the Maharaja and was received by His Highness in full Durbar in the Palace Hall. After Dur-

bar His Honor drove back to his Camp
at the Moti Bagh, witnessed the Gymkhana sports in the evening, and after
dining with His Highness the Maharaja
and the Kour Sahib, proceeded to the
Railway station and there slept for the
night in his saloons.   Early in the morning at 7 A.M., the special train conveying
H. H. the Lieutenant-Governor and party
left Patiala for Nabha.